The Late Arrivals

For Emily and Nicholas

First published in Great Britain by
HarperCollins Publishers Ltd in 1994

A CIP catalogue record for this title
is available from the British Library.

ISBN: 0 00 193952-1

Produced by HarperCollins Hong Kong
This book is set in 16/20 Cochin

The Late Arrivals

MARK BURGESS

Collins
An Imprint of HarperCollins*Publishers*

Introduction

A few years ago Hannah Hedgehog took over the little hotel by the sea from her Aunt Hetty. Hannah's aunt was tired of hotel life and had decided to travel the world in her hot air balloon.

These days Hannah's Hotel is the ideal place for a holiday. Hannah is helped by Molly Mouse; Sam Squirrel is the cook and Rodney Rabbit does all the odd jobs.

Everything is done to make the visitors happy. However, sometimes things do go wrong – such as the time when the racoons came to stay.

"What a time to arrive!" grumbled Rodney.
It was late. Long after dinner.
And now the racoons had arrived.
"They did say that they might
be late," said Hannah.
"I was about to go to bed," said Rodney.
"It can't be helped Rodney, you've got to go
and fetch them."
Rodney,
still grumbling,
went downstairs.
He fetched the torch
from the broom cupboard
and set off for the boathouse.

It was a very dark night.
Rodney didn't like using
the ferryboat in the dark.
He liked to see where he was going.
Rodney lit the lamps, started the engine
and then carefully steered the ferryboat out of
the boathouse. He headed for the mainland
where he could see the lights of a car.

As Rodney got closer, the car headlights began
to dazzle him. He screwed up his eyes to try
and make out the jetty.
"Why, hello," called a voice in the darkness.
Rodney couldn't see a thing. "Can you
switch those things off?" he called.
"What?"
"The HEADLIGHTS!" shouted Rodney.

There was a thud
and a scraping noise
as the ferryboat hit the jetty.
"Bother," said Rodney. Now he would have to repaint it. As if he hadn't enough to do.
The headlights went out.
"Hello," said the racoons. "Sorry we're so late."
"Hmm," muttered Rodney. "Is this ALL your luggage?" There were nine suitcases lined up on the quayside.
"Well, of course, there's
my flute," said Thelma Racoon.
"And my bassoon," said Walter Racoon.
"And my cello," said Franklin Racoon.
"Do be careful with it, won't you."

“Yes, yes,” said Rodney, impatiently.
He stowed the luggage and then helped
the racoons on board.
“Are we really going to cross in this?”
asked Thelma.
“Unless you’d rather swim,” said Rodney.
“Ha, ha. That’s a joke isn’t it? Mr Rabbit
made a joke, Walter.”
“Wonderful,” said Walter Racoon. “This is
all just wonderful.”

Hannah and Molly were waiting to welcome the racoons to the hotel. Rodney struggled up the steps with the luggage.
"Do be careful, Rodney, those are musical instruments," said Hannah.
Rodney was about to say something but then nearly dropped the cello.

"Let me show you your rooms," said Hannah as they went upstairs. "I'm afraid the door to Room 5 sticks a bit. Rodney will fix it in the morning." She gave the door a shove and they went inside.

"My, what a lovely hotel," said Thelma Racoon.

"I wish we could always stay in a place like this," said Franklin.
"Well, I hope you enjoy your stay here," said Hannah. "Sam, our cook, is just preparing a little supper for you which will be ready shortly."
"Why, thank you," said the racoons and they started to unpack their suitcases.

The next day the racoons
were up in good time for breakfast.
"Good morning," said Hannah. "I hope
you slept well?"
"Didn't we just," said Franklin Racoon.
"My, I haven't slept so well in ages," said
Thelma Racoon.
"I slept as if I was in my own bed," said
Walter Racoon.
"Good. I'm so pleased," said Hannah. "What
are you planning to do today?"
"We thought we'd explore the island,"
said Franklin. "There's an old castle,
isn't there?"
"Yes, that's right," said Hannah. "Would you
like a packed lunch? Sam makes excellent
sandwiches."
"That would be wonderful," said Walter.

"There is one other thing," said Thelma.
"We should like to do
a bit of music practice
before we go out.
We wouldn't want
to disturb the other guests,
but we do have the concert
at the town hall this evening and –"
"Oh, I'm sure it would be all right," said
Hannah. "Let me see... the conservatory
should be a good place and don't worry, I
think most of the other guests are going out
for the day."

Dora Dormouse and her old friend Oswald Owl were in the sitting room. They were discussing plans for an inflatable bicycle that they'd invented. Hannah came in to ask if they'd mind if the racoons rehearsed in the conservatory.

"The racoons would like
to practice their music," she said.
"No, I don't like macaroons," said Oswald
Owl, who was a little deaf.
"How interesting," said Dora. "What
instruments do they play?"
"Flute, cello and bassoon," said Hannah.
"Jelly and balloons?" said Oswald. "How
lovely, I do like a party. What are we
celebrating?"
"He doesn't hear awfully well," said Dora.
"Never mind," said Hannah.
"I'll bring you some
coffee and biscuits."

The racoons set up their music stands in the conservatory. Thelma took her flute out of its case, Walter picked up his bassoon and Franklin checked that his cello was in tune. And then they began to play.

"What is that awful noise?" said Rodney as he came into the kitchen through the back door. He put down a basket of vegetables on the draining board.

"That's the racoons practising," said Sam. "They're in the conservatory. I think it's lovely."

"Well I hope the plants like it," said Rodney.

"If they do, *you'll* have to learn a musical instrument!" said Molly. She was helping Sam make sandwiches for the racoon's packed lunch.

"Huh!" said Rodney.

Hannah looked into the kitchen. "Rodney,
I do wish you'd remember
to wipe your shoes.
There's mud
all over the floor."
"Your aunt never minded," said Rodney.
"My aunt doesn't run the hotel anymore,"
said Hannah, crossly. "Oh, and Rodney –
Molly and I are going shopping. We shan't
be back until after lunch. Please will you
sort out the door to Room 5 before we get
back. It's still sticking."
Hannah went off
to get ready.

"Work, work, work," muttered Rodney and he went out, slamming the back door so hard that it made Sam drop a whole pile of sandwiches on the floor.

"Now I'll have to start again,"
said Sam, with a sigh.

"Oh, just wipe off the mud.
Nobody'll notice," said Molly.

A little while later
Sam went back into
the kitchen after having
his mid-morning nap.
The packets of sandwiches
were still lying on the table.
"Oh dear," said Sam to himself,
"the racoons have forgotten their lunch."
He wondered what to do. "I know, I'll take
them to them myself." So he carefully packed
the sandwiches into a bag,
swung it onto his shoulder
and set off for
the castle.

"My, have you come all this way with our lunch?" said Thelma Racoon when Sam had caught up with them.
"That's so kind of you," said Franklin Racoon.

"And we thought we would have to go without," said Walter Racoon.
"Silly of us to forget. Will you have some with us?"
"Err... Ummm... All right," said Sam. They sat down by the castle.

"These are DELICIOUS," said Franklin, taking another mustard and cress sandwich.
"So crunchy," said Walter. "How do you do that?"
"Oh... you know..." mumbled Sam.

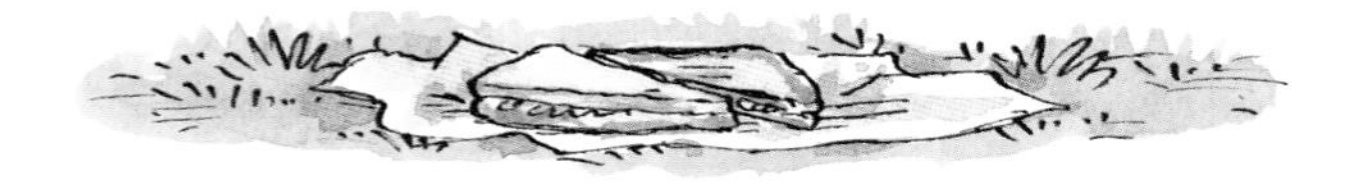

Rodney was watering the plants in the conservatory. He was just thinking how beautiful they looked when he suddenly remembered the door to Room 5.
He must stop it sticking before Hannah got back and it was already half-past two!

Rodney got his toolbox and went upstairs. He gave the door a shove and almost fell into the room. It opened quite easily.
"Well I don't know what all the fuss was about," he said.
Then Rodney noticed the racoons' musical instruments.
He checked that no one was about outside, closed the door firmly and then peeped inside the flute case.
Rodney carefully took out the flute and tried blowing it.

Nothing happened.

Rodney blew a bit harder.
Still nothing happened, so he put the flute back in its case and picked up the cello instead. He plucked the strings with his paw. This did make a noise.
Rodney played what he thought was a nice tune.
He wondered if the geranium on the window-sill was enjoying it. It hadn't wilted, anyway.

Then Rodney thought that he had better stop, so he put down the cello and tried to open the door.

It was stuck.
He gave it a good tug. It wouldn't budge.

“Oh bother,” said Rodney. He had left his toolbox outside. “Help!” he called. “Help!”
Where was everybody?
Rodney opened the window and looked out.
Oswald Owl was walking in the garden.
“Help!” shouted Rodney. “HELP!”
Oswald looked up.

“Help me, will you,” said Rodney.
“You want your bill?” said Oswald.
“No,” shouted Rodney. “I don’t want a bill!”
“Oh, you want the gerbils!” said Oswald.
“Stay there, I’ll go and get them.”
“No, NO!” shouted Rodney, but it was too late. Oswald Owl had gone.

Hannah and Molly arrived back from their shopping trip. They met Oswald Owl in the hall.
"Ah good," said Oswald. "Rodney... err... the gerbils..."
"Gerbils! Where?" said Hannah, dropping her shopping bags.
"What?" said Oswald. "Excuse me, I'm a little deaf."
"WHERE ARE THEY?" shouted Hannah.
"Oh, upstairs," said Oswald.
Hannah and Molly dashed upstairs.

"Help!" shouted Rodney
from inside Room 5.
"Rodney, where are the gerbils?"
said Hannah.
"Gerbils? There aren't any gerbils,"
said Rodney. "I'm stuck in here, that's what."
"Oh, thank goodness for that," said Hannah.
"Is something the matter?" said Thelma
Racoon. The racoons had
got back from
their walk.

"The door's stuck," said Hannah.
"But we must leave for the town," said
Franklin. "We have to give our concert."
"Our instruments are in there," said Walter.
"And we mustn't be late."

"We'll have to break down the door,"
said Hannah. "Stand back, Rodney."
Hannah, Molly and Sam ran at the door.
There was a CRASH!
as it gave way
and they tumbled
into the room.
"My cello!" wailed Franklin Racoon.
The case had been flattened.

"It's all right," said Rodney, twanging
the strings. "I got it out of the way
just in time."

Hannah helped load up the car so that Rodney could drive the racoons to the town hall for the concert.

"Going so soon?" said Oswald Owl.
"They'll be back later," said Hannah.
"A waiter?" said Oswald. "Oh, I used to be a waiter."
"Here's my flute," said Thelma Racoon.
"Now let's go."
"You'd like me to hoot?" said Oswald. "Of course... It would be a pleasure..."